A Centaur's Solstice Wish

Siobhan Muir

SIOBHAN MUIR

DEDICATION

Dedicated to Sage Marlowe because he loves centaurs.

SIOBHAN MUIR

ACKNOWLEDGMENTS

Writing a book is never really a one-person job. In fact, it takes a great deal of hard work, editing, and research on the part of the author to get things correct. Great thanks go to Silver James who made sure my military references were right on and the typo bugs weren't too big. Thanks to Cheryl Dragon for catching more typos (where do these things come from?) and tightening the world concepts to make them clearer. And great thanks to Sage Marlowe for checking my authenticity of the interactions of my guys. Without these folks, this story wouldn't be as smooth as it is.

SIOBHAN MUIR

CHAPTER ONE

Sedgewick stirred awake as the lilting sounds of someone singing filtered into his awareness. He scrubbed his face with his good hand and searched the clinic's confines for the source. The soft radiance from lanterns in around the room gilded the beds and couches set out for the injured. *Like me. Dislocating a shoulder while stringing my bow.* He grimaced in disgust. *I'm a pathetic archer.*

The singing continued, a woman's voice, and he listened for a while, the melody both sweet and plaintive. The lyrics spoke of coming home for 'Christmas', whatever that was, and the tune made him wish for things he hadn't thought of in months. Okay, not completely accurate. *No, more like days.*

Sedgewick rolled to his hooves and rearranged the sling holding his left arm. The shoulder still ached like he'd been stabbed, but at least standing up and walking no longer hurt. He stretched gingerly, extending each hind leg then each foreleg before walking into the community hall. Mare Bethany McMacken, the Master Healer of the Cedarfell herd moved from window to window, stringing garlands of pine boughs. She tied them to each post with red ribbons, singing more about snow and holidays.

Sedgewick stopped and watched her progress, his heart swelling with both joy and sorrow at her singing. She'd found her mate, her love, and her calling despite the disadvantage of being human. Until she'd come through the rift in the dryad lands, he'd never seen a human and always thought them fictional creatures. But she'd not only proved real, she managed to become one of their best healers and a valued member of the herd in spite of her strangeness.

He envied her. *I'm still strange even though I'm a centaur.*

He wanted to find his mate, his love, and his purpose, but he couldn't seem to make anything work. He made a lousy warrior, had very little skill at weapon maintenance, and the one person he loved appeared well beyond his reach. *So far out he may as well be in a different world.* But therein lay the problem. While he hadn't made any overtures toward anyone, he'd never found any mares who caught his eye. *A mare would be far easier.*

He leaned against the windowsill with his good arm and stared out at the wintery night and the softly falling snow. The other members of the original cohort were out there on patrol, shivering their tails off. He liked mares, thought of them as good friends and members of the community, but none of them had ever made him burn with need.

Not like Ronin.

Corporal Ronin Creekjumper with his dark skin, fierce blue eyes, and his dark auburn hair worn long in a thick braid down his back. Sedgewick shivered. The man epitomized beauty with broad shoulders framing a heavily-muscled hairy chest and belly. Sedgewick had often fantasized about Ronin while bathing or tending his herb garden, often getting lost in the daydream to the detriment of his time management. He'd tried to emulate the corporal with his easy strength and agility, but he possessed no soldiering skills, hence why he'd dislocated his shoulder when stringing a bow.

The last thing he'd seen before the pain fogged his sight was Ronin's white appaloosa-blanketed hindquarters as the man turned away from him in disgust. Sedgewick leaned his forehead against the glass as shame washed over him again. *No more disgusted than I was, Ronin.*

"Hey, Sedgewick. How are you feeling tonight?"

Bethany stopped beside his window and gave him a warm smile.

"I'm feeling better tonight, Master Healer. Thank you."

"Oh, you can call me Bethany. It's Christmas Eve. No need to stand on ceremony tonight." She tilted her head with a small frown. "Are you having trouble sleeping? Is the pain bothering you?"

"No, Ma—Bethany." He grimaced at his slip. "I heard you singing."

"Oh, I'm sorry. I didn't realize it had been that loud. I just get into the spirit of the season and lose track of where I am." She shook her head. "I should remember to be quieter."

"No, no, it was beautiful. Peaceful and yet wistful. Are the songs from your home?"

"The Christmas tunes? Yes. Things we used to sing as kids. We'd go caroling from house to house when my mother—my dam was alive." The Master Healer smiled as she set a lit candle down on the windowsill. "It was damn cold, but the singing kept us warm and there was always hot cider or cocoa waiting for us when we got home."

"That sounds like a pleasant memory." He grimaced as his shoulder twinged. "Full of magic."

"It's a magical time of year."

Sedgewick snorted and shook his head. "Not magical, just harder. Colder. Darker."

"That's why we have candles and cheery fires, and after the solstice, the days get longer again." Bethany gave him an understanding smile. "But it can be a lonely time without loved ones." She sighed a little. "I miss my brother most of all."

Sedgewick heard the sorrow in her voice. "Has your brother returned to the Goddess?"

"What? Oh, no. At least, not that I've heard." She shook her head. "I just don't get to see him much, and now, not at all."

"Why is that, Master Healer?"

"He's a soldier, a fairly elite one, and he's always off saving the world. It's impossible to know if he'll be home for Christmas, and most of the time he's deployed somewhere exotic." She snorted with amusement. "The lucky jerk usually gets to go somewhere warm in the southern hemisphere." But her smile fell away. "Unfortunately, he doesn't get to have fun there. He's a sniper." She paused. "Do you know what a sniper is?"

Sedgewick frowned and shook his head. "I'm not familiar with the term."

Bethany bit her bottom lip in thought. "He's really sneaky and quiet, and usually takes the enemy out by long range...bow shots. He's too far away for them to see him."

"That doesn't seem like an honorable way to fight."

Bethany nodded. "No, but it's a good way to keep his team safe and to facilitate rescue operations. He's their backup." She smiled a little. "Still, I send prayers up each year to keep him safe. I'm *his* backup."

"It's good to have brothers-in-arms, or sisters as the case may be, who have your back." Sedgewick turned his gaze out to the snowy night. "I often wish to have such companions."

Bethany raised an eyebrow. "You don't have that now in your cohort?"

Sedgewick shook his head and glowered. "No. I'm a terrible soldier and the other men know it. This injury just confirms it. So I'll just have to go on wishing."

"Where I grew up there's this belief that at this time of

year, magic really happens for those who don't have any." She waved the hand glowing with her healing magic. "I didn't always have this ability, so I don't count. But the saying goes if you make a Christmas wish, the magic of the season makes it come true."

Sedgewick snorted. "You think the Goddess Epona will grant my wishes just because it's snowing outside?"

Bethany gave him a secret smile and shrugged. "I don't know, Sedgewick, but the energy at this time of year is different, more magical and mysterious. I'm sure you can feel it when the land goes to bed under a blanket of snow. But I do know that miracles are known to happen around this time of year. Too many stories about it to ignore."

She winked as she patted his human shoulder and continued lighting fragrant candles around the room despite the lanterns. Sedgewick turned back to the window and considered what she'd said. The snow had slowed and the clouds cleared a piece of sky. The Hunter's Point, the brightest northern-most star, glowed from its little patch of clear sky like a beacon to all those below. He stared up at it, wondering if Bethany knew more than he about the magic of the world than him.

She certainly uses it more regularly.

He sighed and straightened his shoulders as he faced the window, mentally shaking his head at his whimsy, but still incapable of not trying.

Sweetest Epona, Goddess of all the Herds, please hear my prayer. Please let me find my heart's desire tonight. He paused, trying to visualize what that would be. He closed his eyes, imagining himself working on something with great skill and proficiency, enough to garner admiration for his abilities from the community. At the last second as his mind's eyes swung around the crowd, Ronin appeared beside him and wrapped a burly arm around Sedgewick's shoulders, squeezing in a proprietary manner. *Oh, yes, please.*

He opened his eyes and the Hunter's Point winked at him. At least he thought it did, though stars sparkled all the time. *I'm just imagining things.* He swung his gaze back to the room behind him, hoping no one had noticed his little prayer. *It's a silly wish anyway. Ronin is too much a soldier. He'd never notice me.*

But he couldn't get the image of Ronin hugging him out of his head. Sedgewick sighed and turned from the window. He'd be no closer to the soldier if he didn't heal from his disgraceful injury. While he recovered, perhaps he could learn some of Master Bethany's skills at healing. He'd learned some herb-lore from his granddam when he'd been too young to run with the other colts. He'd expanded on the knowledge with some of the more understanding mares. He'd often made tinctures and salves for rashes and cracked skin for the men while out in the field.

The doors to the infirmary barn burst open, scattering garland and making the candles flutter in the snowy air. Sedgewick jumped a little, his tail clamping down on his hindquarters in fright.

"Master Bethany!" Ronin's voice thundered in the quiet space. "Come quickly!"

"Corporal Ronin. What's going on?" Bethany strode through the beds toward the door where Ronin entered with his men who supported two other staggering soldiers.

"Lordy, what happened to them?" Bethany's eyes widened. "Here, bring them over to these beds in the corner. Be clear, Corporal. What happened exactly?"

Ronin grimaced. "They were patrolling under the trees along the northwestern perimeter when Private Navarro stepped into a hole disguised by the snow and steadied himself against a tree. Several lacy-looking creatures dropped onto him and bit him, I guess." He gestured at the red, swollen welts over the centaur's neck and shoulders. A few more ran along his back and haunches. "Private First Class Colver tried to pull him out away from the nest of these things and haul him back to the village, but he was stung as well. Both collapsed within sight of the other sentries and we brought them here."

"Aw hell, looks like they got stung by something poisonous. Please go find Mare Roanie and have her come here. Hopefully she'll know what to do to mitigate the poison."

Sedgewick's mind ran in little circles as he took in the utter beauty of Ronin's form, but a calmer side reflected on the description of the creatures in the forest. *Granddam called those winter lace stars.* She'd told him the nasty little critters often had nests in older trees and were as ornery as hornets when anyone got too close. Their stings couldn't kill anything unless the hapless victim got too many. Then the poison shut down the organs unless an antidote was administered.

The list of ingredients needed and the dose size for each soldier appeared in his mind like a parchment with words written there. Sedgewick raised his head and stepped up to Bethany's side.

"I know what to do, Master Healer Bethany."

CHAPTER TWO

Ronin had never been so glad to see his injured soldier in his life. Sedgewick Icetrotter constituted one of the worst soldiers he'd ever trained, but he'd shown determination and persistence despite his setbacks. When he'd dislocated his left shoulder trying to string a bow, Ronin had seen the defeat in the younger centaur's face along with the pain. Ronin's heart ached for him, but he'd kept his words to himself. *No need to compound his shame.*

Now Sedgewick stepped forward, arm in a sling, with more confidence Ronin than had ever seen him display, and some of his tension melted away. *By the Goddess, let him be able to do this.* Ronin rarely prayed, but he wanted the best for Sedgewick. The man had a gentleness and beauty Ronin had never seen in any other centaur, and some part of him wanted to preserve that. *It would be ruined by fighting and war.*

"What do we do, Sedgewick?" Bethany fixed her green-brown gaze on the buckskin stallion. "Do you know what caused the welts?"

"Yes, Master Bethany. They're called winter lace stars and they have a bad toxin that shuts down the organs if there are enough of them." Sedgewick ran his hands lightly

8

over the welts on Navarro's arm and the man groaned. "We're going to have to make an antidotal salve and smooth it over each of them."

"Do you know what goes into the salve?"

"Yes. My granddam taught me." He grimaced and wouldn't meet Ronin's gaze. "The problem is I can't make it with only one arm."

Ronin gripped Sedgewick's shoulder. "I'll help you. Just tell me what you need done and I can be your extra hands."

Both Bethany and Sedgewick gaped at Ronin for a moment. Hellfire, he'd surprised himself with the outburst, but he wouldn't go back on his offer. His men needed him and he'd do anything he could. *And if you're really honest with yourself, you'd admit you want to spend a little time with Sedgewick.*

Bethany was the first to recover. "Thank you, Corporal. That will be very helpful." She nodded to the injured men. "First, I'll need you to get these men stripped so we can see the extent of the damage."

Ronin stuffed his disappointment behind a sharp nod. "Will do."

"Good. Sedgewick, please show me what you need and let's get started."

While Ronin helped the other soldiers to undress Navarro and Colver, he kept Sedgewick in sight as the buckskin directed Bethany in a soft but sure voice. The men moaned when they lifted their shirts and armor, and he cringed in sympathy. Great, swollen welts spread across their backs from skull to tail, disfiguring them in red sores.

Medicinal scents accompanied the grind of a pestle against a mortar bowl, and Ronin turned just as Bethany called for him.

"Can you please grind this while I prepare the salve base, Corporal?"

"Yes, of course, Master Healer."

Ronin took the pestle as the human woman gave him a friendly smile and he tried to smile back, but Sedgewick's presence beside him made it difficult. *Oh, for the love of Epona, I should be able to do one simple task.* He bent to it, putting his strength and focus into the action of grinding the medicinal herbs. He almost jumped when someone laid a hand on his forearm.

"Firmly, but gently, Corporal. Marble isn't as good as the herbs for healing." Sedgewick's voice held amusement as well as warmth.

Heat blossomed across Ronin's cheeks and chest. "Forgive me, Sedgewick. My concern is with my men."

Sedgewick lost his smile and nodded, releasing Ronin. "Of course, Corporal. But if you grind them too much, they lose potency." Sedgewick nodded to the mortar. "I think they're ready. Bring them to the fire, please."

Ronin regretted his words immediately and cursed himself for a nervous fool, but dutifully followed the buckskin soldier and swept the crushed herbs into a pot of boiling water. Sedgewick nodded and stirred them with a soothing rhythm, his good arm flexing in ways that set Ronin's heart galloping. *Sweet Goddess, what I'd give to feel his arms around me.*

Ronin mentally balked at the uncharacteristically tender thoughts and shook his head. "Must you keep stirring?" The question came out harsh, but Sedgewick smiled.

"Yes. It's necessary to boil them down to their essences." He shrugged. "Long work, but worth the effort."

He stood beside Sedgewick, watching him stir the pot of herbs in a companionable silence. His motions added a level of comfort to Ronin's world, an unusual sensation, and one he'd sorely missed. It reminded him of times spent with his dam while just a wee colt, when she'd ruffled his hair and told him he'd someday find a mare of his own to stable.

Ronin mentally shook his head. Despite his mother's prediction, he'd never been interested in mares or mating. His focus had been on the military life with his brothers-in-arms. He'd striven to be the best soldier and leader to those who depended on him. It had been all he needed.

Until now.

Ronin's gaze rested on the bunching muscles of Sedgewick's arm and an unbidden desire to touch welled up in his chest. Ronin wanted Sedgewick by his side and in his barn, sharing the military life with him. *Even if he does make a terrible soldier.* He took a breath to say something, but an uncharacteristic fear closed his throat. Fear that Sedgewick would find his interest unwelcome. The buckskin stallion had never shown a proclivity for male-male interaction, but Ronin wished for it with all his heart.

Please, Goddess, give me this one chance.

****

Sedgewick tried to keep his focus on the boiling herbs, but Ronin's presence beside him made it difficult. The man smelled like leather, fresh snow, and pine, which complemented the spicy scent of medicinal herbs simmering in the pot. He wished he could bottle the scents and keep them in a keepsake bag to take out when he needed happiness or comfort. To be brutally honest, he'd rather have Ronin's arms around him. *Dream on with that one.* The appaloosa stallion appeared only interested in soldiering and Sedgewick had a distinct lack of ability in that arena.

The admission settled into Sedgewick's gut and his lips pulled down at the corners. All he'd ever wanted was to do something admirable in Ronin's view. But being a remarkable soldier remained outside Sedgewick's capability.

Disappointment took root just as Bethany called to him

from the other side of the room. "I think the salve base is done. How are the herbs?"

"Ready." Sedgewick shot an apologetic look at Ronin. "Can you pour this through the strainer into a bowl, Corporal? She'll need the water to mix in."

"Of course." Ronin nodded sharply and poured the herb mixture through a wicker strainer, the steam adding color to his stubbled cheeks. Sedgewick tried not to enjoy the intense expression on Ronin's face as he focused on pouring the brew.

Bethany appeared on Sedgewick's other side, holding the oil salve base. "I used lavender oil to help with the skin. After we add the herb water, what else do we need?"

"One whole limb of numb spire should be enough for this batch of salve."

"What's numb spire?" Ronin handed the bowl to Bethany and set the pot aside.

"It's a succulent plant like aloe that has properties of anesthetics." Bethany carefully added a little herb water before stirring it into the oil base.

When Ronin gave her a blank look, she grimaced. "Sorry. The point is, it numbs the pain, dulls it to the point where the patient can't feel it anymore." She smiled. "Sedgewick showed it to me a few weeks ago."

"Really?" Ronin raised his eyebrows. "How did you know that, Sedgewick?"

Pleasure heated his cheeks. "My granddam taught me a lot about medicinal plants and their uses. Master Healer Bethany is still learning about our world, so I brought her some numb spire when I hyper-extended my leg."

The memory of the embarrassing episode in his training destroyed a little more of his ego. Ronin had been so disgusted with him, he'd sent one of the sergeants to bring him to the infirmary. *Yeah, definitely not my best moment.* None of the moments in training had been Sedgewick's best. He freely admitted he was only at his best when working with medicines and recovery therapy.

"I'm really grateful. Sedgewick is a treasure-trove of knowledge on centaur medicine." Bethany smiled as she stirred. "Let's add the numb spire and get these men treated."

"Corporal, can you squeeze the spire's pulp into the mixture? The Master Healer must keep stirring to distribute the gel evenly." Sedgewick handed him the arm of the plant and mimicked how to push out the juices. "Start at the top and slide your hand down."

A blush warmed his cheeks as the suggestive nature of his instructions hit his awareness. *Holy Goddess, could I be more bold?* But Ronin did as instructed and showed no sign he'd noticed the intimacy of the statement.

Bethany stirred and Sedgewick kept his attention on the greenish salve, waiting for the consistency to reach the right thickness. It didn't take long with the water, oil, and gelatin reacting to each other.

"That's perfect." Sedgewick dipped a finger into the mixture and brought it to his nose. He inhaled and nodded. "This will do nicely. Let's get this on the welts."

He led the way over to Navarro and grimaced at the state of the sores on the stallion's skin. Ronin swallowed hard beside him and his hands tightened into fists.

"By the Goddess, those things are hideous."

Sedgewick wasn't sure he meant the welts or the winter lace stars, but he had to agree with the corporal's assessment. "Hold the bowl for me, Corporal, and I'll show you how to take care of this."

He dipped his fingers in the bowl of salve and scooped out a liberal amount. "You want your fingers full of salve because you need to completely cover the welts, and you don't want to get any of the poison on your skin." He smeared one of the sores with oily salve while Navarro moaned. "See? Each one must be covered thus." He met Ronin's jewel-blue eyes. "Understand?"

Ronin nodded before switching his gaze back to Navarro's scarred shoulders. He dipped his fingers in the medicine and applied the salve to the man's skin. "Like this?"

"Yes, just like that. The whole thing must be covered or the poison will spread and the healing will take much longer." Sedgewick adjusted Ronin's hand to make sure the red corona around the sting mark held salve. "There. Do each one like that."

Ronin nodded and continued to treat all of Navarro's wounds. Bethany scooped out some of the salve into another bowl, and treated Colver, but Sedgewick couldn't break away from Ronin's side. He told himself he only wanted to be sure the corporal did it right, but in truth, he just wanted to stay beside the chestnut appaloosa stallion. *Dear Goddess, I'm pathetic.*

At last, both men rested, covered in spicy-scented salve. Satisfaction filled Sedgewick, but he fought the exhaustion of his emotional ride with Ronin. Half the time he'd hoped and prayed the corporal would give him an encouraging word or look, and the other half he spent berating himself for hoping. He'd never wanted anything so much as he wanted Ronin, but he'd never measure up to the high standards Ronin held for everyone, including himself.

"That should do it, I think." Bethany laid clean sheets over the sleeping soldiers and headed for her wash basin to clean the oily residue from her hands. "How often should we apply the salve, Sedgewick?"

"In the morning and evening tomorrow. That should tell us how quickly the men will recover."

Sedgewick followed her, reluctant to meet Ronin's gaze. If he did so, the other man would certainly say goodbye and go back out on patrol. Sedgewick swallowed the urge to ask him to stay in tonight.

"How soon would you estimate it will take them to heal, Sedgewick?" Ronin scrubbed his hands under the warm water as Bethany dried hers.

"A few days at least." Sedgewick frowned in thought, trying to keep his eyes away from Ronin's flexing shoulders and arms. *Why does he have to be so beautiful?* "More than likely it will take a week to recover both their skin and their endurance. The poison is hard on the system."

Ronin nodded and sighed. "Nothing more to do than hope and light a candle to the Goddess for them."

Sedgewick blinked in surprise. "You light candles for those hurt or sick?"

"Of course." Ronin nodded. "I lit one for you each time you were injured."

The statement warmed Sedgewick's heart more than it should, but he grimaced. "That must have depleted your candle supply."

Ronin laughed and the candles around the infirmary seemed to brighten for a moment. "I did light quite a few, yes."

"You know, I'm not a soldier myself, but it seems to me you'd make a better medic in the infirmary helping the injured than a fighter, Sedgewick." Bethany leaned against the counter and tipped her head. "I don't know how it works, but if you're interested, I could use your help and expertise here. What do you think, Corporal?"

Ronin smiled ruefully and nodded. "I think that could be arranged. If that's what you'd like, Sedgewick."

Sedgewick took a deep breath. Being a medic under Master Healer Bethany would mean he wouldn't spend as much time with Ronin. But he'd be useful and helpful, and Ronin wouldn't have to light quite so many candles. *I could be with Ronin outside of duty without worries of fraternization.*

"I'd be honored and pleased to work with you, Master Healer Bethany. I don't know how much of my knowledge will be beneficial, but you're welcome to all of it."

Bethany's smile warmed him almost as much as

Ronin's. "Then you should start calling me Bethany. Master Healer Bethany is such a mouthful."

"But—"

"If it's a familiarity thing, call me Healer or Healer Bethany. It's faster and easier." She held out her hand to him and he slowly grasped it around her wrist. "Welcome to the Sagittarius Infirmary, Private Sedgewick."

"Thank you, Healer Bethany." Something clicked inside Sedgewick and he felt settled for the first time since journeying to the Cederfell Herd with Ronin. "It's an honor to serve under you."

Bethany snorted. "You're serving beside me, Sedgewick. We have equal knowledge, just in different areas."

"But you have magic, Healer Bethany."

She nodded. "Only recently and I don't use it unless it's dire circumstances. Most of the healing I do around here comes from what I've learned and observed." She waved her hand dismissively. "In any case, I'll be glad to have another knowledgeable healer with me. Now, it's Christmas Eve and we all deserve some time off. Corporal Ronin?"

"Yes, ma'am?" Ronin drew himself up to attention.

"Private Sedgewick is to report here to the Infirmary, but not until the day after tomorrow. It's a holiday and if your cohort doesn't have to patrol, I don't want to see you until then. Is that clear?"

"Yes, ma'am." Ronin nodded.

"Good. Blessed, holy night to you both. See you at dawn in two days, Sedgewick."

"See you then, Healer Bethany."

Bethany nodded and retreated back to check on the men in the beds. Sedgewick glanced over at Ronin, but the corporal had withdrawn into himself, his expression closed. Sedgewick's heart sank. Had he screwed up again? Did Ronin want him to stay in the cohort? Sedgewick gathered his courage and a deep breath.

"Corporal, is everything well?"

Ronin blinked as if coming back to himself. "Yes, of course, Sedgewick. Come, let's get you situated tonight."

Sedgewick dipped his head in acknowledgment, but some of his earlier confidence slipped. What if he'd chosen wrong? What if this change came as an insult to Ronin? The last thing he wanted was to hurt the corporal. *Oh, Goddess, I only wanted to make him happy. I wish I knew how.*

His spirits dropped as he gathered his jerkin and short cloak then followed Ronin out into the frigid night.

CHAPTER THREE

Sedgewick lapsed into silence as they stepped into the cold, clear night. The snow had stopped and the moon shone down them, painting blue shadows under the trees and buildings. Everything appeared serene and still, but Ronin worried Sedgewick regretted his decision to serve under Master Healer Bethany. *I thought he'd be happy to do something he excels in.* It certainly worked out better for Ronin. Now he could approach Sedgewick with more personal requests without the problem of fraternization within the ranks.

Except he had no idea how.

Ronin stared up at the nearly quarter moon and sent out a fervent wish. *Sweet Goddess Epona, let me have the courage to tell Sedgewick my heart's desire.* Ronin had never wished for anything other than strength in battle, but this night seemed far more important than any military confrontation he'd experienced.

Love wasn't something he'd trained for. His focus had been on warfare. But in the battle for his heart, he felt woefully inexperienced. Ronin shot a look at Sedgewick, but the private's expression remained shuttered and withdrawn. Ronin focused on trudging to the barracks. He had to come up with a plan of action, or he'd lose Sedgewick forever.

His dam's voice filtered through his memories. *To love is to recognize yourself in another, Ronin. How would you like someone to approach you with declarations of affection?*

He'd gotten no closer to an answer when they reached the barracks for the men. Sedgewick strode past the dark forms of sleeping stallions while Ronin waited by the door. What could he do? Before he realized he'd moved, Ronin's hooves carried him to Sedgewick's side and he grasped the buckskin stallion's arm.

"Grab your gear and come with me, Sedgewick."

"Sorry, sir?" Sedgewick frowned, his body tense.

"Grab your gear. You're not staying here tonight with that shoulder."

Sedgewick paused, but nodded slowly. "Yes, sir." He stuffed his belongings into his rucksack and followed Ronin back out into the snow.

Not my most affectionate invitation. Ronin swallowed a grimace and led the way to his own quarters. As an officer, he'd been allowed to build his own barn. It wasn't a large space, not like the barn for Captain Yarren Plainsrunner and his mares, but it retained a comfortable atmosphere and space requirements.

"Where are we going, sir?"

"You're going to stay with me until you report to Healer Bethany." Ronin had no idea where this all came from, but he wouldn't examine it until later. "I need to brief the sergeant on the location of those White Lace Stars and check on the men, but I will return. Please stoke the fire and I shall be there presently."

"You want me to stay with you, Corporal?" Sedgewick's eyes filled his face.

"Yes..." Ronin paused and softened his voice. "Please, Sedgewick. Stay with me until you report to the infirmary."

The buckskin stallion still hesitated. "Are you sure, sir?"

"Yes. Very sure." He stepped closer to Sedgewick, nothing but stars overhead. "I would very much like to share the next two nights with you."

Sedgewick blinked as he clutched his rucksack closer to his chest. "Really?"

Did Ronin hear some hope in the question? "Yes, really." He squeezed Sedgewick's arm gently before releasing him. "Please build up the fire and I'll be there as soon as I can."

"Yes, sir."

Ronin nodded and headed back out to the perimeter, not daring to look back. Sedgewick had sounded bewildered and uncertain, but something deep inside Ronin said he'd done the right thing. *I sure hope so, or tonight's gonna get awkward.*

****

Sedgewick stood in front of the fireplace in Ronin's barn and tried to figure out what had happened. In the space of ten minutes he'd gone from private under Corporal Ronin to a medic under Healer Bethany, and then Ronin invited him to stay. With him. In his barn for two nights. Sedgewick's mind still couldn't quite process everything.

Maybe I didn't mess anything up. He shook his head. *Why would Ronin want to spend tonight and tomorrow with me?* He shot a look at the door to the barn. *Maybe the Goddess heard my prayer.*

The moment he'd stepped inside Ronin's quarters, he felt warm, comfortable, and welcome in the distinctly masculine space. The walls were constructed from simple pine boles covered in resin and nothing else. But a few jewel-toned rugs covered the floor and a sturdy stone fireplace made up most of the leeward wall. Sedgewick caught the flash of mica crystals in the rocks as he knelt to build up the fire. The barn wasn't as large as the barracks, but Sedgewick wouldn't choose to be anywhere else.

With the fire crackling happily in its grate, Sedgewick scanned the room for something useful to do. *What can a one-armed stallion do that's useful?* He found Ronin's kettle and swung it over the fire, careful not to singe the leather-bound handle. That done, he hung his cloak on the hook beside the door and found several candles around the room in lantern jars. He lit a few of them with a piece of kindling from the fire, grimacing a little. *These are probably the ones he lit for me.*

He placed the last one in the window and leaned against the frame, his mind churning with questions. He figured he'd been nothing but a constant source of irritation and disappointment to Ronin. But while Sedgewick's list of shortcomings could fill a stable, Ronin's request to spend the next two nights with him suggested something else.

Oh, please, Goddess. Let it be so.

His breath fogged the glass as moonlight sparkled on the snow outside. If he could have just one wish this holiday season, he'd wish for the chance to tell Ronin his heart. *What I should wish for is the courage to tell him.* Baring one's heart to someone else always came with consequences, but this time Sedgewick had the added fear based on their shared gender.

By the time Ronin returned from briefing the sergeant, Sedgewick's stomach had knotted and he dripped with sweat. He tried to soothe himself by watching the corporal disrobe from his snow gear, but that only excited another part of him, which set off the worry again. Seeking anything to distract himself, Sedgewick removed the steaming kettle from the fire and set about pouring tea.

"Oh, the fire feels good." Ronin extended his hands toward the flames in the grate. "It's bitter cold now that the sky has cleared."

"Are the other men well?" Sedgewick tried to keep the conversation light even while his gut seethed with nervousness.

"Yes. They'll avoid that area for now until something can be done to mitigate the winter lace stars." Ronin shook his head with a grimace. "They're brutal when you get too many on you."

"Yes. Thank the Goddess more weren't injured."

"Thank the Goddess you were there tonight. Colver and Navarro owe you their health."

The look on Ronin's face warmed more than just Sedgewick's cheeks. "I'm very glad I could help. For once."

Ronin chuckled. "You're not as bad as you may think, Sedgewick. You've always had heart, determination, and persistence. I've never doubted your efforts."

"No, but determination doesn't mean skill. I don't think I'm cut out to be a soldier."

There, he'd said it. As much as it stuck a knife in his gut, he admitted he had no skill at fighting. He stared down at the steam curling up from the teacups rather than meet Ronin's gaze. Ronin valued warriors, and Sedgewick would never be one.

"I think you're right. But I don't need more soldiers, Sedgewick." Ronin's soft voice made Sedgewick look up. "I need a medic and a colleague."

A colleague. Sedgewick sighed inwardly. *It's better than nothing, I suppose.*

He gave Ronin a quick smile. "I can do those things, I think. Would you like some tea?"

"Horseapples! That wasn't the right word." Ronin frowned as he scratched his bearded chin. Sedgewick liked the trimmed hair outlining the corporal's jaw. He'd often wondered if it would be soft or wiry.

Ronin raised his cerulean gaze and nailed Sedgewick with a thoughtful look. "I guess the word is friend, but I want more than that."

Sedgewick blinked. "You want to be friends?"

Ronin paused. "Yes...Does that sit well with you?"

"Oh, yes. Yes, of course." In all honesty, Sedgewick wanted more, but having Ronin as a friend was a good place to start. *And I have two nights to convince him otherwise.* He had no idea how he'd do that or where the courage to try had come from, but he wouldn't challenge it.

"Good." Ronin smiled and clapped at hand to Sedgewick's shoulder. "Now, I have something special I'd like to show you. It's something my sire would do with me each year around Solstice." Ronin dug out a small cauldron. "It was our personal version of a dining-in."

A dining-in was a tradition celebrated by the cohort at holidays, a formal meal within the unit for the members only. Sedgewick watched curiously as Ronin cracked several scrub-fowl's eggs and separated the yolks into a separate bowl.

"Here." Ronin handed him the bowl full of yolks. "Stir two scoops of sugar into that."

Sedgewick found the sugar jar and added the recommended amount to the yolks then stirred the best he could. He braced the bowl with his injured hand and beat the eggs as he watched Ronin whisk the daylights out of the whites.

"What are we making, Ronin?"

Ronin gave him a smug smile. "My sire called it Solstice Grog, and it's got a pretty good kick." He lifted up a small glass bottle with golden liquid inside. "I was saving this for a special occasion and I think this counts. How are the yolks?"

"Sweetened, I'd guess."

Ronin laughed and Sedgewick couldn't help but grin back. "Good. Now to add a dollop of this..." He poured a generous quantity of the golden liquid into the sugared yolks and the scent of the alcohol burned Sedgewick's nose.

"Sweet Epona, that's going to kick someone's ass."

"Just watch." Ronin added generous measurements of woolly goat's milk and cream to the sweetened mixture, urging Sedgewick to stir gently. "You don't want to beat it too hard or the cream will thicken too much."

Something else had already thickened with Ronin's hand on his, but Sedgewick tried to keep his mind on the potion they mixed. When Ronin deemed it ready, he carefully folded in the egg whites and took the cauldron outside.

"What are you doing?"

"It must chill for a while before it's ready to drink." Ronin put a lid on the cauldron and closed the barn's door. "Come. Let's make a small supper while we wait for the Solstice Grog to cool."

Sedgewick followed him back to the galley portion of the barn and helped prepare a meal of cold smoked pork, goat's cheese, bread, and odd red fruits Healer Bethany called tomatoes. As he chopped and sliced the food, Sedgewick tried to enjoy working beside Ronin for something other than warfare, but his mind churned with the meaning behind Ronin's invitation.

Sedgewick hissed as he sliced into his finger and cursed his distraction.

"Damn, Sedgewick. What did you do?" Ronin reached for his hand.

"It's nothing. Just a small slice." Sedgewick shifted away, but the corporal caught his shoulder and turned him back.

"Here, let me see." Ronin pulled him around until he could look at the cut. "That's pretty deep. I thought medics were good with knives."

Sedgewick's mood plummeted and he jerked his hand out of Ronin's grasp with a scowl. "I'm not a medic. I'm not a good soldier. Hellfire, I'm not even a good centaur." He clamped his tail tight to his hindquarters and backed away from the corporal. "I shouldn't be here. I should get my gear and go back to the barracks. I don't know why I'm here."

All he wanted was to be with Ronin, but he couldn't do anything right, and Ronin just wanted friendship, nothing more. *Why did he ask me here? I can't do this.* The idea of being stuck in Ronin's barn as just a platonic friend soured his stomach and frosted his mood.

Ronin growled with challenge and crowded Sedgewick against the wall, his face a mask of anger. Sedgewick twisted as his flank hit wood and ducked his head, leaning back until his shoulders met pine. Ronin leaned forward with his arms bracketed on either side of Sedgewick's shoulders.

"You will never, ever, demean yourself in my presence. Is that clear, Private?"

"But, sir—"

"Is that clear?"

"Yes, sir."

Ronin's gaze bored into him as they stood nose-to-nose, and Sedgewick tried to find the patented stoic expression he'd seen on his comrades' faces. But he failed in that, too. *Hellfire, I'm hopeless.*

At last, Ronin sighed and retreated a little, dropping his hands to Sedgewick's biceps. He took a few deep breaths, staring down at their mingled hooves.

"I'm probably not saying this right, but listening to you tear yourself down makes me want to pummel something." Ronin met Sedgewick's gaze with a hard look. "You might not be meant to be a soldier, Sedgewick, but that doesn't make you less than any of us. Soldiers are like pebbles in the river. There are thousands of us. But skilled medics are few and far between. Healer Bethany is a gift...and so are you."

Sedgewick scoffed. "I've only done one thing, and anyone could have helped those men."

"No, not anyone. Healer Bethany didn't have the knowledge, and neither did I." One of Ronin's rough palms cupped Sedgewick's shoulder. "And I've seen you binding the men's minor wounds while in the field. Without that, without you, we would've been a cohort full of injuries."

"Those were little things."

"Every little bit helps—"

"No, they don't." Sedgewick snarled and shoved back at Ronin, his frustration overriding his good sense. The corporal blinked in surprise and released him. "No, they don't. Not when I wanted to impress you. Not when what's most important to you is being the best soldier you can. Not when I wanted to show you the best side of me. But all I did was fail. Hellfire, I can't even prepare a meal."

Crushing despair washed over Sedgewick and leaked out his eyes in frustrated tears. Damn, when had he gotten so emotional? *When I failed at everything I've ever tried to do for Ronin.* He turned away before the other stallion could see the debilitating emotion and clenched his fists as he closed his eyes. *Get it together, stal.*

CHAPTER FOUR

Ronin stood astounded, his hooves rooted to the floor. Sedgewick had wanted to impress him?

"Sedgewick, I don't know what to say."

"I know." Sedgewick's shoulders slumped as he turned away. "You only wish friendship, and I'm truly honored by that, but unfortunately my heart wishes for something else that cannot be. If you help me gather my things, I'll return to the barracks until my reassignment."

Sweet Goddess, he thinks I don't want him. Ronin's stomach sank, but he shoved his concern aside and moved to block the door. "Why didn't you say anything?"

Sedgewick stopped, incredulous. "What could I say? You're my commanding officer and I have non-traditional interests. Between that and the fraternization issues, I chose to stay near you and say nothing." He shook his head. "But now you know and you only want friendship. I can give you that, but I can't stay here in that capacity. Not tonight." He grabbed his cloak and tried to swing it around his shoulders, but the injured arm got in the way. He snarled and wrestled with the cloth, but it only wrapped more around his bad shoulder.

Ronin stepped closer and caught the loose end of the

cloak. "I said the only word I could think of was friend, but I want more than that." He waited for Sedgewick to meet his gaze. "There isn't a good word to describe what I want since we can't exactly mate. But I want what comes with having a mate. "Friend" seems a pallid term for that, but it was the best I could come up with on short notice."

Ronin paused and took another step closer, inhaling the scents of peppermint, cedar, and masculine musk belonging solely to Sedgewick. The man's deep brown eyes opened wider as Ronin closed with him. "Please stay, Sedgewick. Please share the holiday with me."

Sedgewick eyed him for several breaths before he slowly nodded. Ronin's gut relaxed and he helped Sedgewick take the cloak off. "How's your hand?"

The buckskin blinked and glanced down at his hand. "Oh, sore. But the bleeding's stopped." He returned his gaze to Ronin's. "I didn't think there was another centaur like me. Are you sure this is what you want?"

"Yes, I want all that mates have, with you. The respect, the admiration, and the interaction. The—"

"The intimacy?"

"Yes, that, too." Ronin tilted his head with a hopeful smile. "That's why I shared my father's Solistice Grog recipe with you. It's a family recipe and not for outsiders."

Sedgewick raised his brows. "Why didn't you say anything to me before tonight?"

Ronin shrugged. "Fraternization was certainly an issue, but until I met you, I'd never been distracted by domestic pursuits." He grasped Sedgewick's cloak tightly and studied the stitching, inexplicably shy.

"You mean by mares."

Ronin shook his head. "By anyone. The military life was everything to me." He retreated to the wall beside the door and hung Sedgewick's cloak beside his own. A few more hooks and they'd be full. Having Sedgewick's things in his barn warmed Ronin's heart more than he expected.

"And now? What's changed, Ronin?" Sedgewick sounded weary. "I'm not looking for your sympathy or mollycoddling, but I've bared my heart to you. Please tell me I haven't made a mistake."

"No, you haven't. I know I'm not saying this well." Ronin frowned and clenched his fists in hopes he'd squeeze out some coherency. "I never needed anyone until you joined the cohort. Then I couldn't help but notice everything about you. Your kindness, compassion, strength of will despite your repeated failures at being a soldier. Hellfire, Sedgewick, most of those men would have thrown up their hands and turned tail. You never gave up. You impressed the hell out of me."

What more could he say? How could he convince Sedgewick he meant every word?

Ronin took a deep breath and raised his chin. "Leadership has its privileges, but it also has its solitude. It never occurred to me I might be lonely until you arrived. I'm not always observant about the softer side of our herd, but the thought of not having you in my cohort or in my barn after the day's patrol makes me colicky. I...I want you, Sedgewick, as the man I come home to, as the healer who takes care of me, as the friend who warms my barn with his smile, laughter, and...buckskin ass."

Sedgewick's eyes had gotten rounder and rounder until Ronin's last line. Sedgewick grimaced and snorted as he shook his head. He looked away from Ronin, his expression closed and Ronin forgot how to breathe. *Sweet Epona, I think I've lost him.*

****

Sedgewick stared down at his hooves, trying to find what to say. *He sounds sincere.* Did he dare believe Ronin, hardened soldier and male's male, really wanted him? Really preferred stallions over mares? *Could I really be that lucky?*

Sedgewick flipped through all the times he'd served with Ronin. The stallion had never showed favoritism toward any of his soldiers, but he'd been a capable and fair leader, and had never treated Sedgewick differently. *Maybe Healer Bethany was right and the Goddess heard my prayer.*

He raised his gaze to meet Ronin's cerulean eyes, and took a deep breath. *It's now or never to take what I want.*

Before he could utter his response, alarm horns blared throughout the village. Ronin froze, the mask of the soldier sliding into place as he whirled. He threw his cloak over his shoulders and strapped on his weapons. Sedgewick's gut sank, but he reached for his cloak as well, until Ronin stayed his hand.

"No, you're injured. Stay here while I see what this is about. I can't have you out there in the line of fire."

"But Ronin, I can help—"

"No, not this time. You might be needed should there be injuries. Stay."

Ronin threw open the door to his barn and galloped into the night. Sedgewick swore as his gaze followed the chestnut appaloosa until he disappeared into the maelstrom of centaurs gathered in the center of the village. *Be safe...*

The thought brought Sedgewick up short. *Safe? Heh, that stallion couldn't be safe.* It wasn't in his nature. Sedgewick glanced behind him at the candles flickering in the barn and realized he'd make a target of Ronin's home. He threw the door shut and doused all the candles except one. *For Epona and for Ronin.* Something to bring him home.

Sedgewick stood in the warm darkness of the barn and thought about what he could do. With one arm in a sling and poor battle skills, he couldn't go out to fight. *Hellfire, I don't even know what they're fighting.* That seemed rather unprepared, so he returned to the door and cracked it open to study the battle happening outside.

"Holy Goddess of all."

Large, dark shapes bounded through the village, sleek and deadly. Sedgewick caught sight of long jagged teeth and glittering dark eyes of the beasts crashing through homes to terrorize the residents within. *What are they?* Centaur soldiers let out war cries as they notched arrows and swung steel. Mares swung torches and bows toward the attacking creatures, and Sedgewick recognized one of the huge forms loping through the fitful light.

Sweet Goddess, they're dire wolves.

One of the great wolves let out a sinister howl and the others matched it, solidifying Sedgewick's blood. He'd heard about dire wolves, but had never seen one close to their old village before. He remembered his granddam's stories about how the wolves could freeze their prey with their howls and take them down without much fight.

Why are they here now?

Sedgewick's first thought suggested the beasts had some nefarious intent, bent on hurting or killing the people here out of malice. But his logical mind kicked in as he took in the great sprays of snow from the fighters. *They're hungry and we have all this pig meat...*

Sedgewick squared his shoulders before he threw his cloak over them. He knew exactly what he had to do.

CHAPTER FIVE

Ronin snarled at the large wolves streaking through the village, leaping on his men. The initial howl from the Alpha damn near paralyzed everyone while the other wolves tried to ambush them. So far no one had been taken down, but he worried about the non-combatants in the village like Bethany and the other mares. *And Sedgewick...*

He shot a look back toward his barn, but the door was shut and only one candle burned in the windows. *Smart.* Sedgewick had made the barn less of a target. With less to worry about, Ronin focused on the wolves. He'd never seen such large canines, but he'd be damned before he let anyone like Bethany or the injured be killed by the predators.

He launched into a gallop, swinging his sword at the largest beast he could see. The wolf snarled, its dark eyes focused on him as it growled low in its chest. His lip curled in his own battle scowl and he leaped at the creature, slashing with his sword before it could pounce. The wolf waited until the last moment and darted to the side, snapping at Ronin with its long teeth. The canines raked his left flank, but he managed to score the wolf's shoulder with his blade.

They separated and stood back from each other, blood

slowly dripping down both their sides. Ronin evaluated the animal as they circled. The pain in his flank screamed for his attention, but he shoved it to the back of his mind as he scanned the wolf's movements. His sword strike had inhibited the animal's use of its foreleg and it limped, but the injury didn't seem to slow it down. It snarled at him, watching for any sign of weakness he showed.

The only weakness I have is for a buckskin healer with coffee-brown eyes and the scent of cedar.

Ronin gripped his sword tighter as he gathered his energy to launch another attack on his opponent when an eerie howl broke over the village. All the wolves turned their heads toward the north, ears flagged forward. A few heartbeats of silence followed until the howl sounded again. Each wolf launched into motion, adding their own howls to the mix as they loped out of the village toward the north.

Ronin let out a breath he hadn't known he'd been holding and sheathed his sword as he took stock of the village. Homes had been damaged and a few of the men had been injured, but overall they'd survived pretty well. He scanned his own barn again and a cold feeling settled into his gut. Something seemed off.

He strode for his quarters, his hind leg protesting the motion against his injury, but Ronin had to know Sedgewick was safe. The frigid night air stung his throat as he lurched into a trot despite the heavy snow. *Please, Goddess, keep Sedgewick safe.* Ronin burst into his barn, calling for his mate.

"Sedgewick! Sedgewick?" He swung his gaze around the room. The fire had been banked and a single candle burned on one of the sills, but otherwise the barn lay empty.

The cold feeling in Ronin's gut solidified into ice as he noticed the empty hook where Sedgewick's cloak had hung. *Sweet Goddess, where has he gone?* Ronin shot back out into the night, but paused long enough to study the snow around his entry for tracks. A set of hoofprints led off into the darkness, away from the village.

Away to the north.

Dear Goddess, Sedgewick, what have you done?

****

Sedgewick struggled through the deepening snow with the huge ham-hock bouncing awkwardly against his good shoulder. When he'd judged he'd gone far enough to offer the wolves a safe dining area, he tossed the ham as far as he could into the snow and backed away.

He tried to stop his chattering teeth as he looked back toward the village, a bright spot some three hundred lengths away. The sounds of battle carried across the frozen plains and Sedgewick hoped he'd be in time to ensure the least amount of injuries.

Remembering the teaching of his granddam, he took a deep breath and let out the best wolf howl he could muster. It echoed over the hills and snow-covered lands, and Sedgewick shivered with the power of it. Silence followed, all sounds of fighting stopped. *That's good, right?*

He howled again, summoning the wolves out to the feast he'd brought. *Anything is better than feeding on the village. They're just hungry. I hope.* He listened hard, waiting to see if he'd convinced the pack to leave the village.

At first he heard nothing and hoped at least the battle hadn't resumed. But then a new sound carried to his ears and dread followed. The wolves had heard his call and bounded across the snow toward him, their snarls and thudding foot-falls rushing before their bodies.

Oh, hellfire, this might not have been the best idea.

Out here on the plains in the moonlit snow, he had no cover in which to hide. Sedgewick stood exposed and running would only encourage the pack to follow him and bring him down. He'd remembered to strap on his long dagger before he left Ronin's barn, but it wouldn't help much against long canines and claws.

Huge lean shapes of the predators streaked across the plains, their bodies bounding easily through the snow. Sedgewick stood back and braced himself for battle. He'd brought them a feast, but he hadn't figured he'd be on the menu. The dire wolves might have other ideas.

I'm sorry, Ronin. Looks like I screwed up again.

It didn't take long for the wolves to reach his offering, or for them to notice him standing a few lengths away. Sedgewick gripped his dagger and kept an eye on the alpha. It was the biggest and meanest looking wolf of the bunch, with one notched ear and a scar across one eye. Didn't look like the eye had lost any sight, though.

The alpha circled around the ham-hock, his tail low and his hackles up. He kept a wary eye on Sedgewick as the centaur shifted through the snow back toward the village. Sedgewick moved slowly and steadily backwards, keeping the wolves in front of him. They wouldn't hesitate to attack him if he moved like prey.

The other wolves growled and whined, their golden eyes trained on Sedgewick, but he kept his gaze on the alpha. His granddam had warned him to always watch the lead wolf in a pack. The alpha's decisions and actions dictated to the rest. Sedgewick kept moving away from the pig meat while the wolves tracked him, their growls raising the hair on the back of his neck.

Everything seemed sanguine until one of Sedgewick's hind feet hit a patch of ice under the snow and he slid awkwardly in a quick motion. The alpha wolf snarled and howled, and one of the others launched through the snow toward him. Sedgewick swallowed against bile and readied his good arm with the dagger to take the brunt of the attack. *Please give me the strength to make it home alive.*

Before the wolf could reach him, the whistle of an arrow through the frigid air made Sedgewick shiver just before the deadly shaft sprouted from the wolf's shoulder where it met the neck. The great wolf took a nose-dive into the snow, spraying white powder everywhere as it slid to a stop.

"Sedgewick!"

Ronin's voice made tears spring to Sedgewick's eyes, but he didn't dare look away from the alpha wolf. Instead, he kept backing away from the pack as Ronin and several other centaurian soldiers thundered up to him.

"Private, are you well?" Ronin appeared out of breath, his face white with cold and anger.

"Yes, sir, I am. Thank you for your rescue. It was timely."

"What the hellfire are you doing out here?" Anger underlay the question and Sedgewick regretted earning it.

"I meant to draw the pack away from the village with a ham-hock from...the stores. I thought it would save lives." He grimaced as he kept moving backwards. "I just didn't think they'd see me as another food source."

One of the other soldiers snorted with derision. "Typical Sedgewick."

"That's enough, soldier," Ronin snapped and the centaur closed his mouth. "Let's get back to the village, but keep an eye on the pack. We don't want to give them any easy targets."

They moved off, surrounding Sedgewick and bristling with weapons. The wolves growled and snarled, but none made the move to take them on. Eventually, the pack turned on the ham-hock, and the centaurs were able to retreat at a gallop back to the village.

Ronin said nothing to Sedgewick the whole way back and Sedgewick's gut sank. He'd been trying to help in his limited way. He knew he couldn't fight, but he thought luring the pack away from the village had been a good choice. Instead, icy fury radiated from Ronin's body and Sedgewick admitted he'd screwed up again.

Goddess, there's just no hope for me.

The only hope he had stemmed from the time and temperature of the night. Surely Ronin would let him stay until the morning at least. Shooting a glance at Ronin's expression, the hope died a swift and final death.

CHAPTER SIX

Ronin's fear and fury damn near choked him as they headed back to the village. He couldn't even look at Sedgewick for fear he'd throttle the courageous fool. *What was he thinking? He could've been killed.* The idea of Sedgewick lying broken and bleeding in the snow made the bile rise in Ronin's throat.

When they reached the village, he brusquely sent the others off to help with repairs and treat the wounded. Sedgewick turned to follow them, but Ronin blocked his path.

"Not you."

"But if there are injuries, Corporal, I'll be needed to help with them." Sedgewick gave him a surprised look.

"You aren't needed tonight. Report to my barn and when I've dealt with the men, I'll speak with you." He thrust his bow into Sedgewick's hands. "Take that back with you and put it up."

Sedgewick opened his mouth to say something, but thought better of it when Ronin raised his chin and narrowed his eyes.

"Yes, sir."

Sedgewick pivoted and headed for Ronin's barn while

Ronin tried to get a grip on his emotions. *Hellfire and horseapples, he could've been torn apart.* Ronin had never been so frightened in his life. He couldn't lose Sedgewick. Not when he'd just found him and they had a chance to be more than brothers-in-arms.

Ronin shoved his concerns down deep and forced himself to organize the recovery efforts. It gave him a chance to cool down and to focus on productive things rather than the paralyzing fear. His orders might have been a touch harsh, but he wrote it off as exhaustion from the lateness of the hour.

"You want me to take a look at that, Corporal, or will you have Sedgewick tend it?" Bethany motioned to Ronin's flank as she directed a wounded stallion to one of the beds.

Ronin blinked and shot a look over his shoulder. "Oh, I'd forgotten."

But the pain came roaring back with his renewed awareness and he groaned.

Bethany snorted. "I've heard of that happening. Let me at least get it cleaned up and bandaged before I let you go home."

Ronin allowed Bethany to work on him as he tried to channel his anger mixed with relief at Sedgewick's actions. *He was only trying to help.* It didn't reassure Ronin much. He hissed as Bethany swabbed the last of his wound before she taped a bandage to his flank.

"There. I recommend you keep it clean and bandaged as much as possible for the next day or so, to give it a chance to scab over." Bethany washed her hands. "Sedgewick will know what to do and might even take pity on you with some numb spire gel." She gave him a stern look. "Try not to reopen it and rest as much as possible."

"Yes, ma'am."

She snorted. "Yeah, I don't believe you're gonna do that either, but at least I gave you my warning."

At last, everyone had been secured from further wolf

incursions and Master Healer Bethany had the injuries well in hand. Ronin gathered his cloak, finally ready to face Sedgewick without skewering him with a battle spear.

Deep breaths will keep you from killing him.

Despite his best intentions, the moment Ronin stepped into the fire-warmed barn and faced his mate, the fear came roaring back. "What in the name of Epona were you thinking, Sedgewick?"

He expected the private to duck his head, but Sedgewick raised his chin and crossed his arms over his chest. "I was thinking of protecting my village, my friends, and my mate in the only way I could, Corporal Ronin. I couldn't fight, but I could draw the enemy away from our home."

"And you made yourself a target. Those wolves could've ripped you apart."

"And saved all the rest of you!" Sedgewick shot back. "I know I'm useless as a fighter. I've got that part, but I was thinking of everyone else and I wanted to be sure you were safe. I did what had to be done to secure the village, Corporal. I don't regret my actions."

"You put yourself in danger. Do you understand?"

"Of course I understand. That was the point." He glared at Ronin. "What does it matter to you?"

"It matters because I love you!"

Tears of frustration and reaction leaked from Ronin's eyes as Sedgewick blinked at him.

"What did you say?"

"I said I love you, Sedgewick. Dear Goddess, the idea of you torn apart by dire wolves damn near made me lame." Ronin shuffled the last few steps to Sedgewick and threw his arms around the slighter man. "I couldn't lose you now that I've found you, now that the Goddess has granted me this Solstice wish."

Sedgewick straightened a little in his arms. "What Solstice wish?"

"To have the courage to tell you my heart's desire."

Ronin closed his eyes and took a deep breath before he opened them again to meet Sedgewick's curious gaze.

"I love you. I want you, and I need you to stay. Forever, or as close to it as you're willing to give me." He dropped his hindquarters to the floor, ignoring the stab of pain from his flank as he looked up at Sedgewick. He grasped the man's hands as he braced his forelegs to keep from sliding. "Stay with me, Sedgewick. Love me, and you shall have my heart forever. Be my mate in all ways."

Sedgewick raised an eyebrow. "In all ways?"

"All ways, Sedgewick."

Ronin scrambled back to his feet and pulled Sedgewick close until they stood nose-to-nose. He inhaled the wool and cedar scents of his lover, letting them calm his wayward fears.

"In every way you'll let me. I want you safe from harm, or under my protection when I'm not on duty. I want you to warm my barn and my bed." He leaned forward and brushed his lips across Sedgewick's, lost in the tender caress. "Be mine, Sedgewick. Grant my Solstice wish and stay with me."

****

Sedgewick lost his ability to speak. Ronin stared at him with such earnestness and love, he could barely breathe past the lump in his throat. Dear Goddess, had Ronin really said what Sedgewick thought? *Of course he did, you dappled dunce. Answer him.*

Sedgewick cleared his throat as Ronin's hopefulness faded and he tried to smile. "Is this truly what you want, Ronin?"

Ronin frowned and shifted to turn away. "Never mind."

"No, wait, Ronin." Sedgewick caught his hands and

held him fast, pulling him back. "It's just my Solstice wish
is the same. To have you in my life as more than my
commanding officer, more than just my friend. I didn't
think you'd want me with my dismal record as a soldier.
But if you truly want me and don't mind my lack of warrior
skills, then I'm yours, Ronin. Now and until the end of
time."

Ronin scanned Sedgewick's face, and Sedgewick
hoped his sincerity came through. He needed Ronin and
wanted him, he'd just never believed the beautiful stallion
would want him back.

"I truly want you, Sedgewick, and I love you." Ronin
pressed his forehead to Sedgewick's. "Stay with me
forever."

"I love you, too, Ronin. I'll stay." Sedgewick tightened
his arms around the larger stallion.

"Thank the Goddess." Ronin rested his head against
Sedgewick's shoulder.

"Ronin?"

"Yes?"

"Can we have the Solstice Grog now?"

Ronin smirked. "Are you trying to get me drunk?"

Sedgewick laughed. "Maybe, but you said it was a
special treat to share with someone you love. And since it's
Solstice and I love you, it seems like the perfect ending to a
wild night."

"I can think of another perfect ending." Ronin's smirk
morphed into a grin.

The hot, erotic look in Ronin's eyes made Sedgewick
shiver for other more pleasurable pursuits.

"Yes, sir."

"Good, I'll get the grog."

As Ronin retreated out into the snow one last time,
Sedgewick glanced out the window and sent his gratitude
winging up to the Goddess. *Thank you for giving me this
one Solistice wish.* He'd found his heart's true desire and

he'd hold onto it for as long as the Goddess granted him life.

THE END

SOLSTICE GROG RECIPE
HAPPY SOLSTICE

1 dozen large eggs,
1 lb powdered sugar,
1 pint brandy,
1/2 pint peach brandy
1/2 pint dark rum
3 pints milk
1 pint heavy cream.

Separate eggs and beat whites to semi-stiff peaks. Blend yolks and sugar. Slowly stir in brandies and rum. Add milk and cream. Fold in semi-stiff whites. Sprinkle with nutmeg. Serve chilled. Serves 25.

**For a "virgin" grog, add a tbsp of vanilla and/or 1 tsp Almond extract in place of the alcohol.

TAKE THE REINS
RIFTS BOOK 1

Social change is normal for a senator's daughter, but affecting gender politics in centaurs wasn't on Bethany's agenda.

All Bethany Stanton needed was time away to think. She never imagined a walk with her horse might lead her so far from home. When she steps through a rift between worlds at an old archaeological site, she realizes she has bigger problems than marriage to the man of her nightmares. Like a herd of centaurs with distressing views on gender equality and "mythical" humans.

As part of the Supernatural Anomalies Investigative Field Unit, Major Stephen "Mack" McMacken has seen and done more weird stuff than written in a science fiction novel. When called in to track down a U.S. Senator's missing daughter, Mack figures it's more a case of runaway rich girl than supernatural mystery. Until his team finds the portal and he's nearly torched by a dying phoenix.

In a world ruled by mythical beasts, Mack and Bethany find themselves on trial for endangering the centaur village. With the only escape route they know gone, working together to establish their innocence might prove easier than avoiding seductive Sirens and ravenous native beasts.

And then there's the not-so-simple matter of finding a way back home…

OTHER BOOKS BY SIOBHAN MUIR

Her Devoted Vampire (from Evernight Publishing)
Queen Bitch of the Callowwood Pack (from Siren Publishing)
Not a Dragon's Standard Virgin (from Siren Publishing)

Cloudburst Colorado Series
A Hell Hound's Fire (from Three Lakes Books)
The Beltane Witch (from Three Lakes Books)

Christmas I.C.E. Magic (Happy Holidays from the Crescent
Moon Lodge Anthology)
Cloudburst Ice Magic (from Three Lakes Books)

Rifts Series
Take the Reins (from Three Lakes Books)
A Centaur's Solstice Wish (from Three Lakes Books)

Bad Boys of Beta Squad Series
Bronco's Rough Ride (from Three Lakes Books)
The Navy's Ghost (from Three Lakes Books)

The Ivory Road Serial
A Walk in the Sand
Outback Dreams

Coming Soon
Order of the Dragon (Warbler Peninsula #1)
Cloudburst Coffee & Spa (Cloudburst Colorado #4)
Second Chance Succubus

ABOUT THE AUTHOR

Siobhan Muir lives in Cheyenne, Wyoming, with her husband, two daughters, and a vegetarian cat she swears is a shape-shifter, though he's never shifted when she can see him. When not writing, she can be found looking down a microscope at fossil fox teeth, pursuing her other love, paleontology. An avid reader of science fiction/fantasy, her husband gave her a paranormal romance for Christmas one year, and she was hooked for good.

In previous lives, Siobhan has been an actor at the Colorado Renaissance Festival, a field geologist in the Aleutian Islands, and restored inter-planetary imagery at the USGS. She's hiked to the top of Mount St. Helens and to the bottom of Meteor Crater.

Siobhan writes kick-ass adventure with hot sex for men and women to enjoy. She believes in happily ever after, redemption, and communication, all of which you will find in her paranormal romance stories.

Connect with Siobhan online at:
http://siobhanmuir.com
http://www.facebook.com/siobhan.muir.35
http://www.tsu.co/SiobhanMuir
http://twitter.com/SiobhanMuir
http://siobhanmuir.com/siobhans-blog
http://pinterest.com/siobhanmuir.35